Kris Carter

A TREE I CAN
CALL MY OWN

A TREE I CAN CALL MY OWN

LUCILLE E. HEIN

Illustrated by Joan Orfe

JUDSON PRESS, Valley Forge

A TREE I CAN CALL MY OWN

Library of Congress Cataloging in Publication Data

Hein, Lucille E.
  A tree I can call my own.

  SUMMARY: A youngster describes his association with a special apple tree throughout the year.
  [1. Trees—Stories.   2. Seasons—Fiction]
I. Title.
PZ7.H3677Tr   [E]   73-6550
ISBN 0-8170-0605-2

Printed in the U.S.A.

I have a tree—
a tree I can call my own.

My tree is an apple tree
standing alone
in the meadow behind my house.

It is a very old tree.
But the apples from this old tree
smell sweet and taste sweet.

My tree is low to the ground.
I think it stoops because it is old and tired.

My tree has a fat trunk,
so fat I cannot put my arms around it
when I hug it or climb it.

I can reach the lowest branches
by standing on a log that is under my tree.
I grab a branch,
pull myself up,
and climb to a hidden place
        where my tree has made a seat
        just for me.

For a long time I could climb
just to the lowest branches of my tree.

Now I am bigger   up
and taller   up
and stronger   up
and I can climb   up
until I am hidden in the leaves,
lost among red and green apple balls.

This old apple tree is my secret place.
No one sees me.
No one knows where I am.

When I look up through the leaves to the sky,
I am looking up to where God seems to be.
God made this apple tree for me.

Sometimes I think I hear whispering.
Is it the leaves talking?
Is it a bird fluffing his feathers?
Is it God talking to me?

An apple tree is beautiful
any time of the year.
My apple tree is the most beautiful
of all the trees I see from my house.

In winter from the window
I see its twisted trunk
and its branches and twigs
black against the sky and snow.

Its branches beckon me.

I put on coat and cap and boots and mittens
and run across the meadow to visit my tree.
It might be lonely and cold in the snow.

I climb to a low branch.
I jump into the soft snow below.

     Wheeeeeeeeeeeeeeeee!

     The snow flies up around me
     and sparkles in the sun.
     It flies into my eyes
     and I see the world through sparkles.

I watch my tree in springtime.

Each day the buds are fatter
and the higher branches more feathery.

Then one day
the first buds pop open
and uncurl like tiny hands,
and I see tiny leaves.

Pink and white blossoms come with the leaves.
These pink and white blossoms are like

lace
or snow
or cotton
or small roses.

Daddy tells me apple blossoms and wild roses
are part of the same beautiful family of flowers
made by God.

A tiny lump grows from a flower cluster.
This lump grows bigger and fatter,
and soon it is a tiny hard green apple
with its stem where the blossoms were.

In summer
the leaves on my apple tree are soft green.
The tiny apples grow and grow
and look more and more like apples.

The apples are green at first.
I bite one
to see how the first apple of summer tastes.
        It tastes bitter,
        sour.
Then one day
I see a red spot on one apple.
The next day I see red spots on many apples.
Soon the whole tree is full of red and green balls
waiting for someone to eat them.
I like them best when they are red and ripe,
but I sometimes try to eat them
        when they are green and bitter,
        when they have brown spots and warts,
        even when they have worms.

I eat the apples.
My friends eat the apples.
Worms and bugs and insects
    bite and chew and nibble and
    peck the apples.

In the fall
my apple tree is not as colorful
as some trees around my house.

The leaves do not turn red or orange or yellow.
They turn brown and gray and faded green.
They fall like scraps of dry paper,
and the wind pushes them about carelessly.
They are caught in the tall meadow grasses.

Sometimes I wish my apple tree
were dressed in brighter colors in the fall.
I want everyone to notice my tree.

But it does not matter.
I like my tree in
                    winter,
                        spring,
                            summer,
                                fall
because it is the tree I call my own.

I call it my tree.
But this apple tree does not belong to me.
I only pretend it is mine.

My apple tree belongs to birds.
> Robins, sparrows, bluejays like my tree.
> A scarlet tanager visits my tree.
> Sometimes a whoooooing owl
> perches on my tree at night
> and calls to me across the meadow.

My tree belongs to animals.
    Squirrels scurry on the branches.
    Rabbits and chipmunks
    play in the weeds under the tree.
    Field mice hide in the tall grasses.

My tree belongs to insects and bugs and worms.
    Bees dive at the blossoms.
    Bugs crawl on the bark.
    Worms nibble leaves and apples.
    Spiders make webs to catch
    my face and hands.

My tree belongs to people, too.

It belongs to the man who owns it.
    This is his meadow.
    The apples are really his.
    But he lets me call this my tree.

My tree belongs to children.
    My cousin Sara comes to visit me,
    and she cannot get enough of my tree.
    My friends come to play in my tree.
    We pretend we are

                    climbing fire ladders,
                    living in a skyscraper,
                    fishing from a bridge.

My tree belongs to older people.
    My brother and sister still come
    to play pretend games in my tree,
    and they are older than I.
    Mother and Daddy come to my tree
    and sit on the old log under it
    and watch the sun set.

But most of all
my tree belongs to God.

Mother and Daddy tell Sara and me
everything belongs to God.
God gives us everything
to use and protect and love.

Mother says
even if my tree
has few apples
and is old
and may die soon,
I must take care of it and protect it.

Daddy tells Sara and me
we must take care of
       all growing plants,
       all living creatures,
       all people,
because everything belongs to God.

My cousin Sara visits me often.
Sara lives in a city—all cement and tall buildings.
Trees are hard to find in a city.
Sara likes to play in my apple tree.
She hugs my tree when she leaves.

Now—Sara has found a tree
she can call her own!

Yesterday when Sara came,
we ran to my apple tree
and climbed till we could not see
the ground below.
Then Sara told me about her tree.

Sara's tree is a willow tree
in an empty lot near her house
where children are allowed to play.

Sara says her willow tree is low.
Its branches sweep the grass.
Just a jump and Sara can catch
the lowest branch.
Sara says in her willow tree she is hidden
by soft drooping branches that tickle her.

Sara loves her willow tree,
especially in the spring.

I told Sara to look for a tree in the city.
I knew she needed a tree to call her own.

When Sara visits me,
we often play in my tree.

Sara and I like it when there is a soft warm rain.
We run across the meadow to my tree.

My tree is like a tent or an umbrella.
The lower branches and the grass underneath
stay dry for a long time.

We sit on the old log.
> We listen to the rain
> dripping and slipping from leaf to leaf.
> We listen to the birds
> that perch in my tree
> to wait for the rain to end.
> We let a squirrel share our dry place.

We eat apples if they are ripe.

Sara likes the soft drooping branches
on her tree,
and she likes the juicy apples on my tree.

We sit there together
> munching
> > and crunching
> > > and lunching.

Sometimes when Sara is with me,
we take our favorite books to my tree.
We perch on our favorite branches
with the leaves like green curtains around us.

We look at the pictures in our books
and pretend we are in the pictures.

Or we pretend my tree is
          a tent in the forest,
          a spaceship,
          an apartment on the twentieth floor.
Sometimes Mother gives us lunch in paper bags
and we sit in my tree and eat.

Sara tells me how she braids
the thin willow twigs
she finds on the ground under her tree.

I tell Sara about the empty nest
with the broken eggs
at the very top of my tree.

I am glad Sara has her willow tree.

I am glad God made this old apple tree for me—
          a tree I can call my own.